faithgirlz

101 WAYS TO HAVE FUN

THINGS YOU CAN DO WITH FRIENDS, ANYTIME!

From the Editors of Faithgirlz and *Girls' Life* magazine

Other books in the growing Faithgirlz™ library

NONFICTION

Best Party Book Ever!
Big Book of Quizzes
Redo Your Room
101 Things Every Girl Should Know
Best Hair Book Ever

Faithgirlz Handbook
Faithgirlz Journal
Food, Faith & Fun: A Faithgirlz! Cookbook

DEVOTIONALS

Finding God In Tough Times
No Boys Allowed
What's a Girl to Do?
Girlz Rock
Chick Chat
Real Girls of the Bible
My Beautiful Daughter
Whatever!

Girl Politics
Everybody Tells Me to be Myself But I Don't Know Who I Am
You! A Christian Girl's Guide to Growing Up

BIBLES

NIV Faithgirlz! Bible
NIV Faithgirlz! Backpack Bible

BIBLE STUDIES

Secret Power of Love
Secret Power of Joy
Secret Power of Goodness
Secret Power of Grace

FICTION

The Samantha Sanderson Series
Samantha Sanderson at the Movies (Book One)
Samantha Sanderson on the Scene (Book Two)
Samantha Sanderson Off the Record (Book Three)
Samantha Sanderson Without a Trace (Book Four)

The Good News Shoes
Riley Mae and the Rock Shocker Trek (Book One)
Riley Mae and the Ready Eddy Rapids (Book Two)
Riley Mae and the Sole Fire Safari (Book Three)

From Sadie's Sketchbook
Shades of Truth (Book One)
Flickering Hope (Book Two)
Waves of Light (Book Three)
Brilliant Hues (Book Four)

The Girls of Harbor View
Girl Power
Take Charge
Raising Faith
Secret Admirer

Boarding School Mysteries
Vanished (Book One)
Betrayed (Book Two)
Burned (Book Three)
Poisoned (Book Four)

Check out www.faithgirlz.com

ZONDERKIDZ
101 Ways to Have Fun
Copyright © 2016 Red Engine, LLC

Requests for information should be addressed to:
Zonderkidz, 3900 *Sparks Drive SE, Grand Rapids, Michigan 49546*

ISBN 978-0-310-74613-3

Done in association with Red Engine, LLC, Baltimore, MD.

Zonderkidz is a trademark of Zondervan.

Editors: Jacque Alberta and Karen Bokram
Contributors: Katie Abbondanza and Patricia McNamara
Cover and interior design: Chun Kim

Printed in China

15 16 17 18 19 20 21 22 23 24 /DHC/ 15 14 13 12 11 10 9 8 7 6 5 4 3 2 1

CONTENTS

CHAPTER 1 • JUST FOR Y-O-U

CHAPTER 2 • HAVE A BLAST WITH YOUR BFF

CHAPTER 3 • FRIEND ZONE

CHAPTER 4 • MINI MAKEOVERS

CONTENTS

CHAPTER 5 • SUPER SLEEPOVERS

CHAPTER 6 • THROW THE BEST BASH

CHAPTER 7 • FUN WAYS TO MAKE $ FAST

CHAPTER 8 • GET ACTIVE

CHAPTER 9 • GET CRAFTY

Never be bored again! Our collection of 101 fun things to do will help make your downtime even more meaningful. Whether you have just a few minutes, a half an hour or a whole afternoon, we're revealing tons of secrets to using your time wisely (good-bye, endless hours idled away on the Web). We'll show you how to bond better with your BFFs, shower your family with sweetness and treat yourself to a some much-deserved R&R.

Plus, we're dishing on how to get creative when you're stumped for gift ideas or just want to whip up some new accessories or bath goodies for every friend on your list. Why is having the right kind of fun under the sun (or in your living room) so important? Learning how to manage stress and use your time wisely—yes, crafting counts as moments well spent!—can help you stay happy and healthy in the long run. Once you start ticking these activities off your after-school bucket list, you'll get a better sense of, well, you. Enjoy!

— *the editors*

JUST FOR Y-O-U

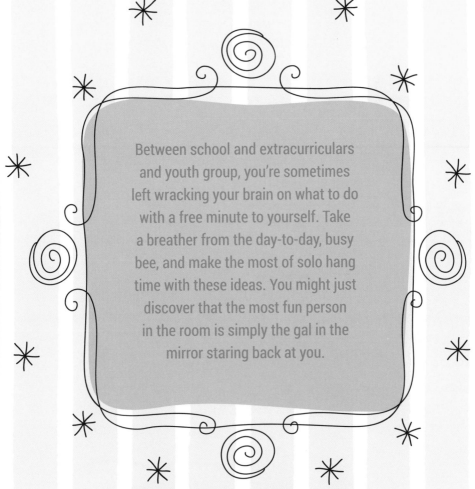

Between school and extracurriculars and youth group, you're sometimes left wracking your brain on what to do with a free minute to yourself. Take a breather from the day-to-day, busy bee, and make the most of solo hang time with these ideas. You might just discover that the most fun person in the room is simply the gal in the mirror staring back at you.

CHAPTER 1

WRITE LOVE NOTES

An insta pick-me-up: Grab your Post-its and start jotting down positive things you heart about yourself.

WHAT YOU NEED

* Post-it notes
* Pen
* Positivity ← *Most important!*

To get started, try completing these sentences...

"I love that God gave me _____."

"I am proud of my _____."

"My _____ makes me happy."

Stick your notes on the mirror, inside your favorite book, or even behind the closet door for feel-good surprises everywhere you turn.

TAKE A BITTY VACAY

Regrouping after a hectic day is as easy as taking a mental getaway. Create a "Quiet Zone" in your room then sneak in, close your eyes and envision a locale that makes you blissfully happy. Maybe it's camp (hello, Navajo cabin reunion!). Maybe it's your grandpa's lake house or that white sandy beach you've only seen on your laptop's screen saver. Whatever and wherever it is, mentally pack your bags and spend 10 savoring every sight, scent and sound. Feeling better already, aren't you?

WHAT YOU NEED

* Peace and quiet
* Thoughts of your favorite destination

STUFF LOVE IN THIS DIY ENVELOPE

Fold a piece of cardboard up 4 inches from the bottom and 3 inches from the top, overlapping the top flap over the bottom. Glue the 4-inch sides together and let dry. Slip your positive note inside the envelope, close shut and secure with ribbon.

BONUS: START A SILLY THANK YOU BOOK
Grab a blank notebook and start writing mini thanks to life's less appreciated things that can't actually receive a card, like that toothpaste you just bought or your umbrella that safely protected you from a downpour. Pen them as they come to mind and read them back for a chuckle when you're having a blah day.

WHAT YOU NEED

* Cardboard, cut in 8 ½" x 11" pieces
* Hot glue gun (ask parent for permission)
* Festive ribbon in polka dots, stars or plaid patterns

FIND YOUR INNER SPARK(LE)

Ignite those internal fireworks by embracing outer sparkles. Start by painting your nails in glitter nail polish (it's great for covering up that otherwise chipped mani). Then use the polish to decorate your favorite accessories like bobby pins, an old pair of sunnies and a plain plastic headband. Wear them all at once or throw each into a rotation. Either way, get ready for your confidence to shine!

WHAT YOU NEED

* Glitter nail polish
* Bobby pins
* Old sunglasses
* Plastic headband

SURPRISE A THANKS

It's important to vocalize the things you're thankful for—and we're not just talking about the ah-dorable charm bracelet you were gifted last week. Surprise the most unsuspecting of people with a bit of written gratitude. Loved that veggie pizza the lunch lady whipped up in the caf? Write about it and share it with her when checking out in line next week. Adore those elderly neighbors who take nightly walks by your house? Thank them for inspiring you by tucking a note in their mailbox next chance you get.

WHAT YOU NEED

* Thank you card
  (turn to page 123 for ideas)
* Pen

CREATE AN ABSTRACT SELF-PORTRAIT

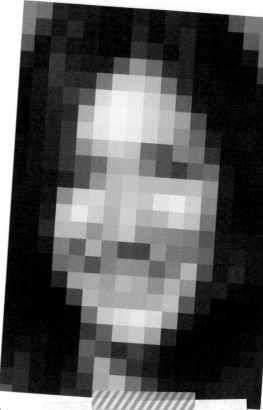

Take a good look at yourself, be it in the mirror or from a photo. Make a mental note of your face shape—is it circle, oval or square?—and its varying colors caused by shadows.

Sketch your face shape on paper (don't stress about your drawing abilities!). Using a ruler, make a grid of 1" squares over the shape. Flip through magazines and look for colorful pictures that you like, or cut pieces of colorful paper into 1" squares. Aim to match the actual shades of your face—so if you have blue eyes, cut squares from a picture of the ocean or blue paper to use as the color around your pupils.

When you've cut out enough squares, start gluing them onto your grid. Voilà, a self-portrait even Van Gogh would admire.

WHAT YOU NEED

* Sketch pad or drawing paper
* Drawing pencil
* Eraser, ruler, glue
* Scissors
* Magazines
* Colored paper
* Mirror or fave photo of yourself

BECOME A VOICEOVER PRO

WHAT YOU NEED

* Audio recorder (or download a recording app on your phone)
* Your favorite book

Uniqueness is one of the many cool things about your voice. And with the right tone, you can make just about anything sound hilarious. Actors make their careers—and mega bucks—out of simply manipulating their vocal gifts.

Ready to try? Pick a paragraph from your favorite book. Record yourself reading it aloud in your everyday voice. Next, reread and record the paragraph using an accent (like an English brogue), followed by a scary voice, a baby's voice and more.

So, what to do with your new skills? Volunteer to read at your library's kid's hour or at a nursing home so patients can enjoy books without straining their eyes. Or just bust out your best princess voice the next time you're reading fairy tales to your babysitting charges. Oscar-worthy!

CHOREOGRAP

OUR TUNE

Determine what type of dance works best with your favorite jam. Is it something slow? You'll want to opt for ballet moves like pirouettes and graceful arm motions. Fast-paced? Stick with a hip-hop routine of lots of leg work and loads of fierce attitude.

Listen to the song one time through with your eyes closed, picturing yourself dancing to the music while focusing on the way the song makes you feel.

Play the song back, this time writing down the lyrics in groups of 4 to 8 lines, and identify the moods of each group. Next, create specific moves for the lyrics in counts of 8 to reflect those moods.

For the chorus of the song (the group of lyrics repeated multiple times in between verses), create a specific set of moves and be sure to repeat each time it's sung—that will give your routine some nice cohesion.

Keep practicing until you have it down, and don't be afraid to throw on a costume (make sure you can dance in it!) to get fully immersed in the music. Just remember that the whole point is to let loose and enjoy yourself rather than worry about forgetting a step.

Invite your fam into your living room to showcase your work. You never know, it might come in handy during your next school dance or talent show!

WHAT YOU NEED

* Your favorite song
* Notebook
* Pen
* Creativity
* Costumes
  (hey, if it helps get you in character, why not?)

BECOME A FLASH FICTION AFICIONADO

Writing something is way more fun when you're not getting graded on it, right? Tap into your inner author by creating a piece of flash fiction (a super short story that can range from just a few words—like 50—up to 1,000).

First, dream up your main character, focusing on one cool thing that makes her—or him—special, like a super cool skill or awesome trait. You want the character to be relatable to others, but still stand out amongst the crowd.

Create a few plot points (like a beginning, middle and end) and get typing. You might just be on your way to becoming the next hit YA author.

HERE ARE A FEW PLOT IDEAS TO GET YOU STARTED:

- Princess Josephine is forced to marry the wrong prince + Discovers animals can now talk...and they have lots to say + At a shoe store

- Budding circus juggler Kyle + Wakes up to a mysterious egg about to hatch + In an ancient castle

- You + Find a time capsule that holds a big secret about the past that could drastically impact the present + At the grocery store

WHAT YOU NEED

* Computer
* Creativity

BE A LIFESAVER

Adding lifesaving techniques to your arsenal not only boosts your employability (hello, new baby-sitting clients!), but it can make you a superhero in serious situations. Put your free time to good use by training on cardiopulmonary resuscitation (CPR) to revive someone who has stopped breathing and the Heimlich maneuver to rescue a person from choking. Check with the American Red Cross (visit redcross.org) to find upcoming classes in your area. Then take pride in knowing you're actually learning something that could help many...and save a life.

WHAT YOU NEED

* A First Aid class

WHAT YOU NEED

* Local tourism guides
(go online if there isn't a
visitor center nearby)

* Camera

* An open mind

HAVE A STAYCATION

Home is where it's happening—seriously. And opening your mind to new experiences evokes the same feeling of an easy-breezy vacation—without the stress of packing a bag or hopping a flight.

Sure, you can use the Web to come up with a million options—but check out paper maps (wait, there's a lake just six miles from you?), newspapers (a yard sale with first-edition novels? You're *in*) and word-of-mouth (ask your youth group buds for the coolest restaurants they've been to lately), then dream up your perfect itinerary. Look up things you've wanted to check out, like art exhibits or free concerts, or find stuff you've been meaning to try, like a yoga class or hiking trail.

Once you've gathered your list of ideas, map out an itinerary for your weekend, determining how you'll get from point A to B to C (some options include a parent, public transportation or riding your bike).

Snap pics of every destination and, in true tourist fashion, don't forget to pick up a souvenir. The great thing about doing this all solo—as long as your parents are cool with it—is that you're bound to meet new people, see something rad or at least get a crazy story out of the deal.

····· INSTA VACAY! ·····

{ RISE 'N' SHINE }

Want a fun way to wake up happy? Grab a wet washcloth and sprinkle it with a few drops of eucalyptus. Stash it in a Tupperware and put in the fridge at night. Whip it out in the morning for a soothing jolt across your face.

{ TAKE A BREATHER }

Indulging in the sweet scent of vanilla can help you instantly chill out. Add a bit to your smoothie or afternoon chai tea. Light Mom's sweet-smelling candle. Its calming properties will subconsciously make you feel great.

{ TWILIGHT ZONE }

Take your p.m. bath sesh to the next level. Mix 2 to 5 drops of essential oils (we heart lavender for its calming effect) with a tablespoon of whole milk and pour into the running water of your almost-filled tub. "Soak" it all in...

HAVE A BLAST WITH YOUR BFF

She can rattle off your Starbucks order, finish all your sentences and predict your mood before you even open your mouth. Sometimes hanging with your forever friend is cool when it's just the two of you doing absolutely nothing. But it's also fun to grab your best girl and try out these activities guaranteed to keep your twosome tight.

CHAPTER 2

THROW A JUST BECAUSE SURPRISE

Celebrate your bestie any day of the week! Stuff a handful of colorful confetti (you can grab some at your local party store) in the envelope and hide it in your bag. When she least suspects it, like on your walk home from school, whip it out and dump it over her head. Surprise!

WHAT YOU NEED

* Small envelope
* Handful of colorful confetti

Shhh...
This is for your eyes only!

COMPOSE A HIDDEN NOTE

Have a secret only she can find out? Write it in a letter—with invisible ink!

Dip your paintbrush into a bowl of diluted lemon juice (add a bit of water to the juice to get it to an inky consistency). Grab your sheet of white paper and write out what you want to say with the brush, then let the note dry.

Tell your bud to read the note by blowing hot air from the hair dryer over the sheet of paper. In no time, she'll see the top-secret info as it turns brown on the page.

Offer up the leftover "ink" for her to scribble a secret back. Just remember to discard the paper when finished...or risk your dog digging up the dirt.

WHAT YOU NEED

* White paper
* Paintbrush
* Lemon juice
* Water
* Small bowl
* Hair dryer

30 MINUTES

HOLD A WEEKLY WALK 'N' TALK

There's nothing better than sweating a little while you get caught up. Find a day and time during the week that works for the two of you and pick a central location in your neighborhood to meet. Walk for 30 minutes while chatting about what's on your mind (and remember: the conversation should be two-sided, so make a point to listen as much as you gab) and let the smiles (and exercise glow) flow your way.

WHAT YOU NEED

* Comfy shoes
* Honesty

SHOP VINTAGE

A new-to-you piece is one way to make your wardrobe stand out, so invite your bud to a day of specialty shopping: thrifting! Grab your list of vintage stores in the area and get browsing. The keys to scoring a fab find? Patience, creativity and an open mind. Seek multipurpose pieces (like a blazer or black dress) that could work with endless outfits. Bonus points for items with durable materials (like tweed or suede) that will last forever.

Feeling extra adventurous? Style an entire ensemble using all vintage pieces. And don't be afraid to hit the dressing room to model off your treasures—it's all about finding the perfect fit.

The beauty of used goods is that each has a story behind it: So even if you walk away with nothing, make up tales about where each piece came from while perusing the racks. A free smoothie goes to the gal who invents the most outlandish legend.

CASH IN BFF COUPONS

It's the gift that keeps on giving. Craft IOU coupons out of construction paper that include "good for one" treats special to your bud. Staple them together to make a booklet that she can tote around and whip out at any time. Have your bud make a book, too, and see how long you can keep the selfless tasks alive.

Some of our fave BFF Coupons...

- Good for one ice cream and chat fest (my treat)
- Good for one math tutoring session
- Good for a week of good morning and good night texts guaranteed to make your day

WHAT YOU NEED

* Construction paper
* Scissors
* Magic markers
* Stapler

DO A WARDROBE MAKEOVER

WHAT YOU NEED

* An all-access pass to each other's closets

Head over to your BFF's house and look through her closet. Put together complete outfits from top to bottom (including accessories and shoes!) that you think she'd look great in. Just remember: the ensemble should be something she's never worn before. Have her do the same to your wardrobe and vow to wear your new creations on the same school day. Give your new stylist credit when the compliments come rolling in.

BECOME (FIT

WHAT YOU NEED

* Comfy workout gear
* A cleared-out space where you can move (like your backyard, open living room, or even the beach!)

FRIENDS FOREVER

We're walking proof that working out with a bud boosts the fun factor. Our trainer friends (and real-life besties) Karena Dawn and Katrina Scott shared these go-to partner circuits.

LINKED LEG SIT-UPS

Sit across from your partner with your legs interlocked (one set of legs will be on top and the other should be underneath, using your feet to "lock" the position). Lie on your backs. With your arms behind your head, use your abs to rotate left and right while rising up to a seated position. At the top, clap hands with your partner and twist back to how you started. Repeat 15 times (going both left and right).

SIDE LUNGE FOR TWO

Stand facing your pal, each with your feet together, arms extended and holding hands. Keeping your knee in line with your ankle and the opposite leg straight, lunge to the same side. Remember: Avoid locking your knee or risk injury. Tighten your abs and push yourself back to start. Repeat 20 to 30 reps on each side. Bonus points if you get through the whole set without LOL-ing.

HIGH-FIVE PLANK

Start in a push-up position. Tighten your abs and high-five your BFF, slapping opposite hands to make it a little more challenging. Keeping your body as stiff as a board, alternate between hands and repeat 10 times. If that's easy, repeat 20 to 30 times.

BELLY BUSTER

Lay on the ground with your friend, feet near each other's shoulders and arms out to the side. Using your abs, lift legs to a 90-degree angle (you'll look like "L" shapes). Slowly lower your legs halfway down and return to start. Next, use your abs to lift your rear end off the ground and move it a few inches to one side. Lower down and repeat 20 to 30 times.

LEAN ON ME PUSH-UPS

Kneel to the ground, keeping your knees about shoulder-width apart. Have your BFF stand behind you and hold your ankles. Contract your abs and lean forward, gently falling into a push-up position. Lower down into the push-up, then explode back up to start. Repeat 10 to 20 times, then switch positions.

ONE
HOUR
OR MORE

DIRECT YOUR MINI BIOPICS

Let your legacies live on in digital form with your nearest and dearest telling your life stories from their eyes. Split apart from your bud for a bit, but complete this same task. Grab a recording device and ask your families and other friends to illustrate the timeline of her life, including funny or inspiring stories that reflect your bud being, well, her.

Start with those who have known her from the beginning (like her parents) and work your way up through friends she's met along the way. In terms of settings, think of the major milestones in your BFF's life: the house she grew up in (including the tree she loved to climb as a kid), the church parking lot where she first learned to ride a bike, the school auditorium where she gave her first class president speech.

Upload the files to your computer and edit with the software of your choice, highlighting the most poignant scenes with music she loves. The final step? Debut your flicks during a viewing party with your families.

WHAT YOU NEED

* Smart phone or any other visual recording device

* Computer

* Video editing software like Windows Movie Maker or iMovie

* A list of those closest to you and your bestie

BURY A BESTIE TIME CAPSULE

Pulling together a cute and crafty collection of your fave moments is the perfect way to document your BFF status. On white paper, scrawl down some memories of the two of you (like that time you broke personal records in the charity 5K last spring) and place them in the box.

Grab some of your favorite photos and trinkets while reminiscing about the items as you add them one by one. Once you've put the lid on it, decorate the outside of the box with your nicknames and favorite code words.

The great thing about this capsule is that you don't have to dig around in the dirt to walk down memory lane. Have one of your parents "bury" it in the closet or attic, then agree on a future date (like your 18th birthday) to "dig" it out.

WHAT YOU NEED

* Shoebox
* White paper
* Colored markers
* Printed pics of the two of you
* Notable mementos like ticket stubs, post cards or playbills

FRIEND ZONE

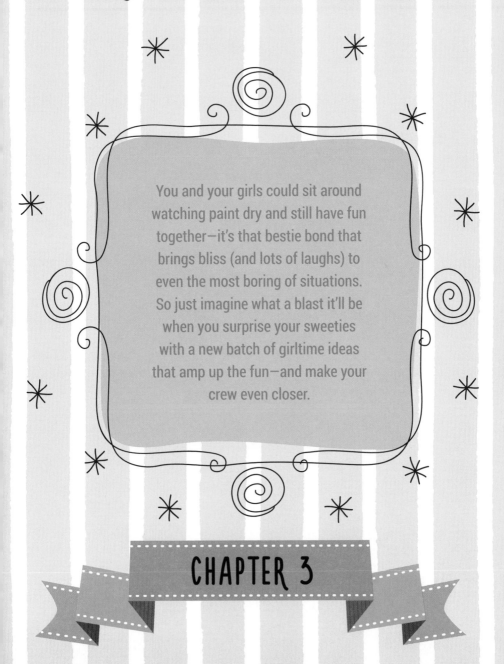

You and your girls could sit around watching paint dry and still have fun together—it's that bestie bond that brings bliss (and lots of laughs) to even the most boring of situations. So just imagine what a blast it'll be when you surprise your sweeties with a new batch of girltime ideas that amp up the fun—and make your crew even closer.

CHAPTER 3

MAKE UP GOOFY PREDICTIONS

No need to bite into a cookie for these. Grab a pad of paper, rip sheets into shreds and have everyone write a funny prediction like "You will adopt a pet hippo" or "You will travel to 20 countries in the next decade." Put them in a teacup and pass around the table. Have each bud pull one out and laugh together at what you've dreamt up.

WHAT YOU NEED

* Pad of paper
* Pens
* Teacup

E-MAIL A FUN FRIDAY TREAT

As our fave *Toy Story* song goes, "You've got a friend in me." Help your buds kick off the weekend by sending out a new bestie-themed YouTube video each week. Don't worry: If you run out of videos (though we doubt that will happen), send everyone a funny meme or link to an article that reminds you of your friendship.

WHAT YOU NEED

* An ongoing scroll through YouTube
* Your friends' e-mail addresses
* Smartphone or computer

DREAM UP A FLASH MOB SING-ALONG

Take door-to-door caroling up a notch—and make it year-round. Invite your friends over for a quick brainstorming session to decide which song you want to perform. It's summertime? Opt for a tune like Katy Perry's "Firework." For the winter months, pick a classic carol.

Plant yourself in a public space like a food court or park. Have your bravest bestie start with the first line of the classic, then pick up the song, one by one, 'til you're all belting it out. Encourage the crowd to join in on your cheerful tune. Now that's music to everyone's ears.

WHAT YOU NEED

* List of seasonal songs
* Your best vocal chops

PARTAKE IN AN ALL-YOU-CAN-WEAR CONTEST...THEN THROW A CLOTHING SWAP

WHAT YOU NEED

* A stash of cute clothes and accessories from each party attendee

Invite your friends over for a fashionable fête where everyone gets a free new wardrobe.

To prep, each girl should scour her closet for awesome items she can trade. Anything goes: Grab dresses, belts, coats, denim, bags, whatever. Hair accessories and jewelry make great trading pieces, too. Remember that you'll be parting with these items...but going home with rad replacements.

When it's party time, pile on as many items as you can. Layer tops over tanks, rock leggings under jeans (with a dress on top!) and load up on jewels. When everyone arrives, take turns counting how many articles each girl was able to rock. The winning fashionista scores the first shopping selection!

Lay everything out nicely (like a boutique), then take turns shopping the stash. Every girl gets to go home with as many new items as she brought. Divvy up any leftovers or donate them to Goodwill. Fashionable up-cycling is so stylish.

PLAY A BOARD GAME MARATHON

Power down for a bit by digging out the classics—Clue, Scrabble or Candy Land, anyone? Have your pals bring their stash and set up games all over the room while you break into pairs or teams. When you're finished with one game, simply move on to the next while keeping scores to determine the ultimate champ(s).

Once you're bored with your, heh, board games, create your own! Grab your poster board and markers and get drawing. Come up with a set of rules and personalize each player's piece by taping printed pictures of each bud to the front of nail polish bottles or bent paper clips.

When you're done, you can always flip the board over and create a bonus game. How's that for some serious competition?

WHAT YOU NEED

* Every board game you can find
* Poster board
* Markers
* Individual printed pics of your friends

HERE ARE SOME TOPICS TO TRY BLOGGING ABOUT:

LIT CHICKS – Books, books and, yep, more books

FRIENDS FOREVER – Any and everything that pertains to BFFs

FOOD FOR THOUGHT – Recipe ideas and reviews of your latest bites

THRIFT SHOPPERS – Style advice for girls on a budget

WHAT YOU NEED

* Laptops
* Camera
* Items related to your theme
* Tumblr account (ask your parents for permission first)

HOST A POP-UP BLOG

O f course your crew has a ton in common...so why not share your interests with the world? Get parental permission, pick a topic and name for your blog, then have everyone haul over their laptops and theme-related items.

Devote a night to making the best-ever Tumblr account on your chosen topic. Have a blast posting quick articles, mini quizzes and funny snaps from your cameras and reblogs.

As repetitive as we might sound, just remember to be careful what you put online. Your blog, like pretty much anything else on the Internet, can be seen by everyone—so be proud of what's on the page.

MAKE A 411 BOOK

One loves sushi, another's all about homemade meatballs. The problem is you can't always remember if it's Alyssa or Tessa. Kylie digs puggles...or is that Hannah? Sometimes it's hard to keep track. Store the scoop on your closest pals in one convenient place.

Take your blank notebook and decorate the cover together so it represents all of you in an artistic way. You can sketch, doodle, collage—whatever you love. Make the first page of the book a sign-in page, where each friend writes her name next to a symbol (like a soccer ball or handbag) that best represents her.

Then, on the top of each page, write a specific question and have each girl answer, using her symbol as an indicator for who she is. Need suggestions on what to ask? Try these:

* If you could only eat one meal for the rest of your life, what would it be?
* What's the coolest gift you've ever received?
* Which color best represents you and why?
* What's one thing another bud has said to you in the past that still keeps you laughing?

Fill the last page with a bunch of hilarious "Would You Rather" Qs (like "Would you rather dye your hair permanently purple or have a permanently blue tongue?") and have everyone write their answers.

Store the book in a safe place and pass it off to another girl on her birthday so, eventually, it circulates through everyone's hands.

WHAT YOU NEED

* Blank notebook
* Materials for your decorations—try decals, stickers and puff paint
* Pens

EMBARK ON A TO

We've got a secret—can you keep it? Scavenger hunts are key to a totally fun bud bonding session.

Make a list of local landmarks and funny activities players must complete (like a "bunny ears" picture with a mailman). You can also list general, easy-to-find items (like a take-out menu) or go extra sneaky and plant obscure items around town (like a face-up penny in a fountain).

Each item on the list gets a different point value—so the harder something is to find, like a pup with a purple collar, the higher the points.

Arm each team with a tote to help lug their findings to the finish line. The team who returns with the most points wins!

KNOW BEFORE SHOUTING "GO!":
EXTRA HELP. If you're dreaming up the agenda, you can't play yourself. Frankly, we think that's just as fun, but if you want in on the action, ask Mom, Dad or one of your older sibs to organize everything instead.
TEAM BUILDING. It works best if you have at least 3 teams with 3 to 5 buds per

ECRET SCAVENGER HUNT

team. That's not to say you can't do it with fewer friends—or more. Just make sure each team has an equal amount of players.

LOUD AND CLEAR. Each team should get one copy of a guide that lists each challenge and its point value, plus any rules.

BOUNDARY BREAKDOWN. Make sure that everyone is aware of the boundaries and what areas are off limits. For example, teams can only search from your house to your pal Angela's. For safety reasons—and straight-up fairness—check that at least one member from each team is familiar with the area before starting.

SNAP HAPPY. Make sure each team has a camera. They'll need to take pictures of certain landmarks or tasks as proof.

SPECIFIC LIMITS. To keep things fast-paced and fun, set a time limit for the event with specific start and end locations (like your front porch). Ready, set, go!

OFFICIAL COUNT. Enlist your "judge" to help check everyone's challenges, tally up points and declare the winning team.

WHAT YOU NEED

* List of knickknacks and to-do activities
* Camera
* Reusable shopping bags

INDULGE IN A DOOR

ONE
HOUR OR MORE

BONUS
There can never be too many cooks in the kitchen! Break each course into teams; one group of buds helps cook the soup in one pal's house, while another group works on the main dish. Delish.

O-DOOR FOOD FEST

Bring your appetite! First choose a yummy cuisine like Italian or Mexican, then divvy up different courses among the cooks in the crew. For example, one bud makes soup, another whips up a salad, while another handles the main dish and another does dessert. Make sure each recipe fits the theme.

Each chef prepares and serves the food at her house. Pick a start time (say, Sunday at noon) for your full crew to show up for the first course. Everyone eats together, then helps clean up. When you're done, move on to the next house for the next course, and so on, until you're stuffed silly.

TIP: While we're all about walking any chance we get, sometimes friends' houses can be far apart. If you can't walk there, ask a parent or two for carpool help.

WHAT YOU NEED

* Full use of your—and your buds'—kitchens
* Delicious food

• 'TIS THE SEASON •

Make Your Own Holiday

Why wait for the big ones to throw a celebration? Dream up festive days with your friends. Let these silly celebrations ideas inspire you!

FROSTING FRIDAY. Because, let's be honest, it's the best part of a cupcake anyway.

"HEY" DAY. Say "hey" to as many new people as possible.

SING-A-LONG SUNDAY. No one's allowed to talk—they have to sing. La la LOVE it!

MINI
MAKEOVERS

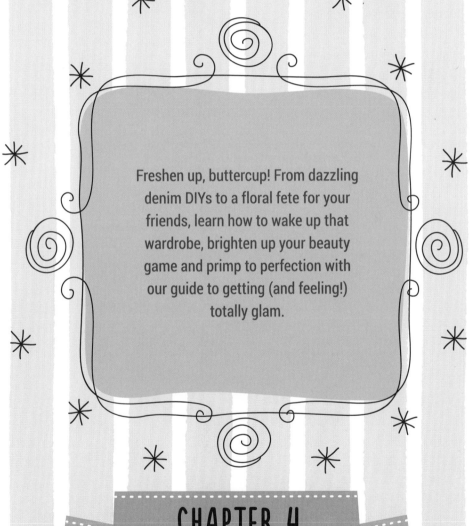

Freshen up, buttercup! From dazzling denim DIYs to a floral fete for your friends, learn how to wake up that wardrobe, brighten up your beauty game and primp to perfection with our guide to getting (and feeling!) totally glam.

CHAPTER 4

10 MINUTES OR LESS

SCRUB A DUB

Scrubs are a speedy way to morph your shower into a spa. Our favorite recipes don't even require a how-to. Just dump everything into a bowl, mix and buff up. Save the rest in a Mason jar and enjoy all week.

WHAT YOU NEED

* 2 teaspoons ginger (powdered works!)
* 1 cup honey
* 3 tablespoons fresh lemon juice
* 2 cups brown sugar

SWEET LIKE
BROWN SUGAR SCRUB

COMING UP
ROSE SCRUB

WHAT YOU NEED

* 1 ¼ cup coarse sea salt
  (try Pink Himalayan salt
  for a pretty hue)
* 6 tablespoons fine
  sea salt
* 3 tablespoons jojoba oil
* 6 drops rose
  essential oil
  (add this last, after mixing
  all of the above)

WHAT YOU NEED

* ¾ cup fine sea salt
* ¾ cup granular
  brown sugar
* ¾ cup almond oil
* ½ teaspoon cinnamon
* ½ teaspoon pumpkin
  pie spice
* ¼ teaspoon ginger
* A few drops of vanilla

SPICED GINGER SCRUB

FAKE IT 'TIL YA MAK[E]

We're all about letting your true self shine through, but sometimes it's fun to play around with new looks without a permanent commitment.

FAKE A BOB

Brush mane into a low ponytail near the top of your shoulders, then pull out any loose pieces from the front and sides. Roll the ponytail up and under, then pin securely. Finish with spray.

WHAT YOU NEED

* Brush
* Ponytail holder
* Bobby pins
* Strong-hold hairspray

FAKE SOME BANGS

Use comb to create a deep side part. Grab a 3-inch chunk of strands on the bigger side, then push it over your forehead to create the "bangs." Secure with bobby pins (or try a big, bold barette). Finish with hairspray.

WHAT YOU NEED

* Comb
* Ponytail holder
* Bobby pins or barette
* Strong hold hairspray

WHAT YOU NEED

* Hair chalk
* Flatiron

FAKE FUN HAIR HUES

For a chic style statement or special occasion, hair chalk is the perfect way to experiment with new hues. The best part? It washes right out with one to five shampoos (depending on your hair color and texture).

Snag hair chalk at a drugstore or beauty supply shop. Want to go DIY? Pick up a pack of soft pastels from the craft store.

To apply, follow product instructions or rub the chalk onto dry hair. Brush out any excess, then spritz with hairspray and seal with a flatiron.

For a natural look, add ombre ends a few shades deeper than your normal hue. Want to go bold? Try bright, standout streaks.

NAIL THE PERFEC

You + nail polish = endless possibilities. Try our top four picks, and then get cute and creative with your prettiest paints.

PUNKY PASTEL

We can't stop talking about this electric nail art that our faves from the website The Beauty Department dreamt up for us.

Apply metallic polish to all 10 digits and let dry. Place the tape in a zigzag pattern on each nail (narrow side in). Paint over entire nail and triangles with pastel shade. Wait 30 seconds, then peel off tape while polish is still wet. Let dry, then seal with a swipe of top coat.

WHAT YOU NEED

* Metallic nail polish
* Pastel nail polish
  (try mint green)
* Painter's tape cut into
  narrow triangles
* Clear top coat

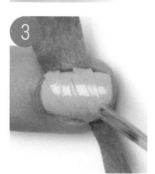

PREPPY PLAID

Another funky-yet-classic design from our go-to nail guru, Hannah Lee.

Start with two coats of gray polish and let dry. Paint a thick white vertical line slightly off-center on each nail with a striper brush. Then paint a thick horizontal line with the striper close to each nail's base. Outline white stripes with black striper, then add another black line down the middle. With red striper, add two accent lines on the opposite side of each nail bed down and across the nail and let dry. Finish with top coat.

WHAT YOU NEED

* Gray, black and white nail polish
* Thick striping brush
* Thin striping brush
* Clear top coat

30 MINUTES

PEDI PERFECTION

WHAT YOU NEED

* Tub of warm water
* Your fave sweet-smelling shampoo
* Cuticle remover
* Towel
* Orangewood stick
* Foot file
* Lotion
* Nail file
* Nail polish remover
* 8 cotton balls
* Base coat
* Your fave nail polish color
* Top coat

Sometimes it's sweet to act like you're hanging at the salon without dropping a dime. This at-home pedi will have you starting any part of your day—or night—on the right foot.

1 Remove old nail polish. Add a couple squirts of shampoo to your tub of warm water and soak your feet for a solid 10 minutes. Dab on a bit of cuticle remover to your nails.

2 Rinse your feet and dry with a towel. Then use an orangewood stick to push back cuticles and a foot file to get rid of any rough patches.

3 Rinse feet and apply a thick layer of lotion. Square off nails with a file and swipe with polish remover once more to nix any trace of lotion or oil.

4 Separate toes with cotton balls. Apply a base coat, polish and top coat. Let dry. Remember: Keep your feet in flip-flops to nix potential smudges.

WRAP UP YOUR HEADPHONES

1. Cut a length of each floss color that's at least two times the length of your earbuds cord.

2. Tie ends of floss together and knot directly below volume button on the cord. Tape earbuds in place on a flat surface while you work.

3. Separate one string from group and pull diagonally to the left. Cross tail of individual string over top of group of strings so it makes a "4" shape.

4. Tuck tail behind group and through hole of the "4," pulling tight to make a knot. Repeat at least 10 times or more, then switch strings and repeat steps 3 and 4.

5. For individual ear cords, cut two strings 3' long. Tie ends together. Knot ends around base of earbud, then wrap strands around cord in a twisted pattern.

6. Tie knot and trim ends to finish. Coat ends with clear nail polish to avoid fraying. Dry, and then rock out.

The only thing more fun than blasting your fave band on the ride to school? Listening to them with spruced-up 'buds.

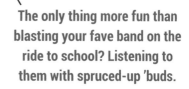

WHAT YOU NEED

* Earbuds
* Embroidery floss in four different colors
* Scissors
* Tape
* Clear nail polish

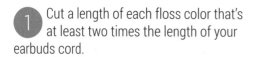

MASK IT

WHAT YOU NEED

* Fork
* Small bowl
* 1 egg
* 1 tablespoon honey
* Splash of almond or jojoba oil
* Herbs (like rosemary)
* Damp, hot towel

Hello, luscious locks! Using the fork, beat the egg in the bowl. Add the other ingredients. Carefully apply to damp or dry hair (make sure you're wearing an old tee). Once strands are coated, wrap up your hair in a damp, hot towel. Let the mask treat your tresses for 15 minutes and then rinse thoroughly. Wait at least another 15, then shampoo.

DO UP YOUR

Got an old pair of blues collecting dust at the bottom of your closet? Give them new life as a genius pair of jean shorts. Rock these stunners all summer long and then pair them with tights during the cooler months.

1 Put on jeans. With the chalk, mark the point where your middle finger hits the side of your leg (ask your mom to help if it's too hard to do it alone). Take jeans off and use a tape measure to determine the number of inches from the outside seam to the mark of chalk. Add 2 to 3 extra inches to accommodate a cuff. Write down that number...that's where you want to cuff.

2 Turn your jeans inside out (this will help you avoid cutting through pockets). Extend tape measure along outside seam again to desired length and mark with chalk. Then use the measuring tape to create a straight, dotted chalk line across the leg.

3 Using a pair of sharp scissors, cut across the dotted line. Repeat all of that on the other leg.

4 Wash and dry shorts, turn them right side in and cuff at the bottom.

And then you can get creative...

≪≪≪≪≪ **WHAT YOU NEED** *≪≪≪≪≪*

* Old pair of jeans
* Measuring tape
* Chalk
* Heavy-duty scissors

DENIM

LACE IT

1. Lay your shorts on a flat surface. Cut a section of lace large enough to fit over the front panel of shorts, avoiding pocket and following seams.

2. Use straight pins to hold fabric in place while you snip for a perfect fit.

3. Thread needle and hand-sew sides of fabric panel, stitching fabric to denim while wearing a thimble to avoid poking yourself. Remove pins as you work. When finished, tie knot and trim ends.

WHAT YOU NEED

* 1 yard lace fabric
* Straight pins
* White thread
* Needle
* Scissors
* Thimble

FRINGE IT

1. Use fringe trim to measure seam along front pockets of shorts and cut to fit.

2. Line pocket seam with a stream of glue and let sit for 3 to 5 minutes.

3. Apply strip to glue, pressing firmly to affix. Let dry and repeat on opposite side.

WHAT YOU NEED
* 12-inch fringe trim
* Scissors
* Liquid fabric glue

WHAT YOU NEED

* Glass bowl
* 2 tablespoons vitamin C powder (or citric acid)
* 2 tablespoons cornstarch
* ¼ cup baking soda
* 3 tablespoons light oil, such as almond, canola or sesame
* 2-5 drops food coloring
* 2-5 drops scented oil (we love lavender or lemongrass)
* Packet of sugar flowers (the kind you'd use for decorating a cake)
* Spoon
* Sheet of waxed paper

DIY THE ULTIMATE BATH BOMB

1 In bowl, mix together the vitamin C powder, cornstarch and baking soda. Slowly add the light oil and stir until you have a soft, dough-like substance. Add food coloring and scented oil.

2 Take small scoops of dough and roll to form balls 2 inches in diameter. Push a sugar flower into the top of each ball, making sure the petals are at the same height as the bomb.

3 Place the orbs on a sheet of waxed paper. You'll have to give them 24 hours to harden and dry before plopping them in your bath (we recommend 2 balls per soak session) or storing them in an airtight container.

CONCOCT SIGNATURE PEPPERMINT PATTIE SOAP

WHAT YOU NEED

* A few small, plastic molds in mixed shapes (like clean sour cream containers or travel soap dishes)
* Brick of white, scent-free glycerin soap (grab it at the craft store)
* Plastic bowl
* Peppermint extract
* Vanilla
* Red food coloring
* Toothpick
* 8" x 8" squares of sheer fabric (depending on size of your soaps)

REPURPOSE SUMMER STAPLES

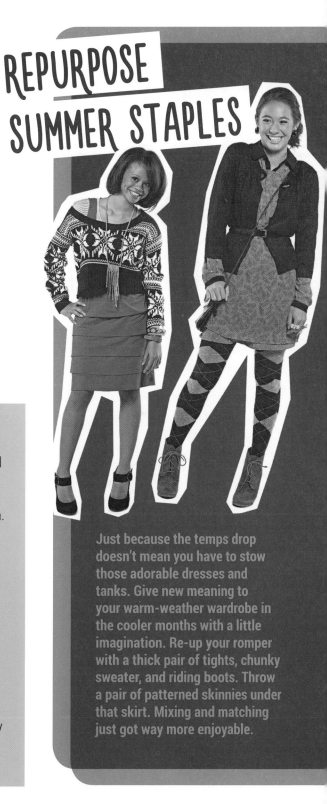

Minty soap will energize your mornings and take less than an afternoon to make. Briliant!

1 Break soap into chunks and put in a plastic bowl. Microwave on high for 30-second intervals until fully melted. Add several splashes of peppermint extract and a few drops of vanilla.

2 Pour about one inch of the mixture into each plastic mold. Put in a drop of food coloring and stir slightly with a toothpick to create a swirly effect.

3 Let soaps harden before removing from molds.

4 Wrap up in sheer fabrics and tie at the ends. Place in your bathroom for a deliciously sweet-smelling treat any time you suds up.

Just because the temps drop doesn't mean you have to stow those adorable dresses and tanks. Give new meaning to your warm-weather wardrobe in the cooler months with a little imagination. Re-up your romper with a thick pair of tights, chunky sweater, and riding boots. Throw a pair of patterned skinnies under that skirt. Mixing and matching just got way more enjoyable.

BLOOMING BFF SPA DAY

Pamper your pals (and yourself!) with this floral-themed afternoon. Have everyone come dressed in their prettiest pastel ensembles, light some rose-scented candles and test out these delicate delights.

ROSEWATER ICED TEA

We sip this sweet floral treat, brewed by Faithgirlz! *Best Party Book Ever* author Jessica D'Argenio Waller, any chance we get.

1. To make rosewater syrup, bring 2 cups water and the sugar to a boil, stirring occasionally. Lower heat and simmer for about 5 minutes. Remove from heat and let cool to room temperature. Stir in rosewater.

2. Fill the other saucepan with 2 cups water and bring to a boil. In the meantime, tie strings of teabags to the handle of your wooden spoon. Once water boils, turn off heat and add tea bags, laying the spoon across the rim of the pot, and let steep for 5 minutes.

3. Pour tea into large pitcher, adding 2 cups cold water and ice to fill. Sweeten with your rosewater syrup, adding 2 tablespoons at a time to taste. Stir and refrigerate for 1 hour. Serve over ice.

WHAT YOU NEED

* 2 small saucepans
* Wooden spoon
* 6 cups water
* 2 cups sugar
* 2 tablespoons rosewater (get it at a health food store)
* 2 bags caffeine-free black tea
* Large pitcher
* Ice

ROSY CUPCAKES

1 Mix cupcake batter in one bowl according to box instructions, adding 1 tablespoon of rosewater to the liquid ingredients before combining with dry ingredients. Bake as directed, until golden and a toothpick comes out clean. Cool completely.

2 In other bowl, cream the shortening and butter with the electric mixer. Add 1 teaspoon rosewater, then gradually add the sugar. Use a spatula to scrape the sides of the bowl, making sure all of the sugar is incorporated. Slowly add the milk and beat at medium speed until the frosting is light, fluffy and slightly stiff.

3 Once your cupcakes are completely cool, use a butter knife to spread frosting over the top. Pile on and swirl to your heart's content.

WHAT YOU NEED

* 2 large bowls
* Electric mixer
* 1 box of your favorite white cake mix (plus all required ingredients, as listed on box)
* 1 tablespoon plus 1 teaspoon rosewater
* ½ cup solid vegetable shortening
* 1 stick butter, softened
* 4 cups confectioners' sugar
* 2 tablespoons milk
* Spatula
* Toothpick

ROSE-HONEY MASK

Our friend Jody Berry, the founder of Wild Carrot Herbals, shared this recipe for petal-soft skin.

1 With your parent's help, heat honey in the double boiler (don't let the honey boil, though!). Pour warmed honey over petals in jar, and use chopstick to stir and get rid of air bubbles. Let the mixture infuse in a warm, dry place for two weeks.

2 The day of the party, gently heat the mixture until warm and strain through cheesecloth into a small bowl. Apply to your face for 10 minutes and rinse.

WHAT YOU NEED

* Jar of slightly wilted organic rose petals
* 8 ounces honey
* Double boiler
* Chopstick
* Cheesecloth

SUPER SLEEPOVERS

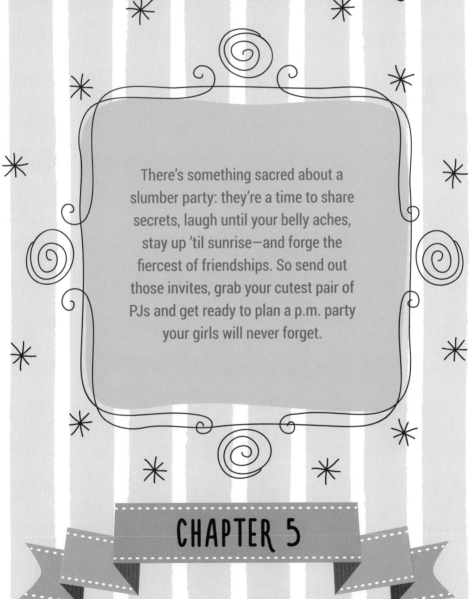

There's something sacred about a slumber party: they're a time to share secrets, laugh until your belly aches, stay up 'til sunrise—and forge the fiercest of friendships. So send out those invites, grab your cutest pair of PJs and get ready to plan a p.m. party your girls will never forget.

CHAPTER 5

START A BOOK SWAP

Ask each of your girls to bring a lesser-known volume she loved (but can part with) to the sleepover. Sit down in a circle and pass the titles around until everyone has something she's never read before. It works well with DVDs, too.

WHAT YOU NEED

* Your favorite obscure book

Bonus!
To up the fun, ask Mom to bake the treats with you beforehand. There's something sweet about hearing her stories of whipping up those same snickerdoodles with her own mother.

INDULGE IN A COOKIE SHARE

Swap some family stories—and sweets. Have each guest bring a tin of her favorite cookie, concocted from a special family recipe, and pass them around 'til everyone has a sampling of each one. Then give each girl three minutes to channel her inner Food Network star and tell everyone how she made them. Guests go home with any leftover sweet treats—and a new set of recipes.

WHAT YOU NEED

* Tin of treats from a family recipe
* Printed recipes

PLAY THE DREAM GAME

Hot potato takes a dreamy twist with this Q&A. Inflate your beach ball and write a bunch of dream-related Qs on it (think: "What's your dream job?" "Who's your dream crush?" or "What's your dream vacay?"). Start some music and toss the ball around in a circle. Whoever has it in her hand when the tune stops has to answer the first question she sees on the ball, then exits the game. The last person left wins.

WHAT YOU NEED

* Inflatable beach ball
* Marker
* List of dream-inspired questions
* Playlist of songs cut in 15- to 45-second increments

love

Friends

friendship forever

Smile, Laugh, Live

SCRAPBOOK THE MEMORIES

Don't let life's highlights sit in a shoebox, collecting dust! Stick them in a memory book you can create during your sleepover.

Have everyone bring photos and mementos and organize by grade, place or event. Assign each friend to a few specific pages.

Using paper, create cut-out shapes that go with the page's theme. For example, you adore all of your ice skating adventures? Snip out a pair of skates, stick it on a photo-safe page and place pics from your rink adventures around it. You can pop your snaps onto funky borders created from patterned paper before securing them on the page, too.

Use your markers to write theme-specific words or dates, and add more depth to the page with stickers. The more shapes and colors you have on each page, the more it will pop.

Leave room for future memories. Place any leftover pics into a handmade pocket inside the back cover of your book.

WHAT YOU NEED

* Hardcover scrapbook with blank, photo-safe pages
* Photos and any other paper memories from your finest moments as friends
* Colored, patterned, and textured paper
* Photo-safe stickers and sticky tabs
* Markers, glue and scissors

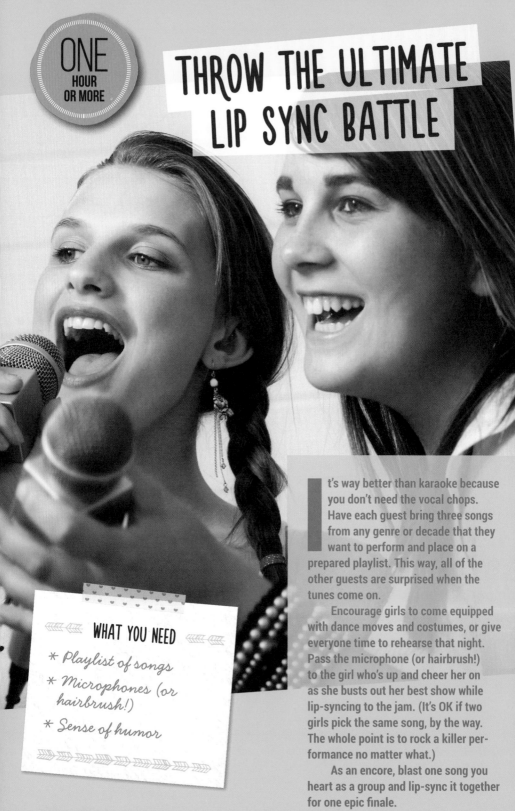

THROW THE ULTIMATE LIP SYNC BATTLE

It's way better than karaoke because you don't need the vocal chops. Have each guest bring three songs from any genre or decade that they want to perform and place on a prepared playlist. This way, all of the other guests are surprised when the tunes come on.

Encourage girls to come equipped with dance moves and costumes, or give everyone time to rehearse that night. Pass the microphone (or hairbrush!) to the girl who's up and cheer her on as she busts out her best show while lip-syncing to the jam. (It's OK if two girls pick the same song, by the way. The whole point is to rock a killer performance no matter what.)

As an encore, blast one song you heart as a group and lip-sync it together for one epic finale.

WHAT YOU NEED

* Playlist of songs
* Microphones (or hairbrush!)
* Sense of humor

HOST A TRAMPOLINE CAMP OUT

We love a sleepover that's filled with junk food and doing nothing more than chilling on the couch. But that's not the only way to bond with your BFFs. Let your girls know you're planning an event-filled sleepover. When they arrive, hand each girl a healthy juice or seltzer spritzer. Then go for a hike in your town or try a bike ride on a local path. Follow it up with a seasonally-inspired dinner, like veggie burgers in spring, huge salads in the summer or turkey chili for early fall. Your movie pick should be sports themed (we like the classic *Bend it Like Beckham*). Then drag the sleeping bags to the trampoline to chat under the stars. (If it rains, just sleep inside on your yoga mats!) In the a.m., serve whole wheat waffles or quinoa with maple syrup. Everyone will leave feeling refreshed and energized...as long as you made sure to actually catch some zzz's!

WHAT YOU NEED

* A friend with a trampoline
* Sleeping bags
* Good weather

MOVIE MARATHON IT

No sleepover is complete without endless hours spent enjoying your favorite flicks. Switch things up by picking a theme for said viewing pleasure. Can't find the DVD of a certain film? Check out the library or try streaming sites like Netflix and Amazon.

* * * * * * * * *

Here are some of our go-to themes:

Hello, Retro – '80s and '90s to the max

Around the Globe – Foreign films for the young at heart (with subtitles, of course)

Girls Rule the World – The best chick power picks imaginable

A Cinderella Story – Animated, comedy, drama...the princess in all her forms

BONUS: Serve up flick-inspired munchies in the middle of your marathon. Minion cake pops, anyone?

More sleepover fun!

TWILIGHT ZONE

NAME THE STARS

Who needs sleep when you can gaze at the sky? Grab a bunch of empty picture frames and head outdoors for a constellation-naming contest. Have each girl hold up her frame to the sky and look for stars inside it that create a familiar object. When each girl finds one, have her come up with a clever name. Hey, it might land in the International Star Registry soon.

RISE 'N' SHINE

SNEAK A SUNRISE SURPRISE

Your girls might not show it, but they'll love it. Set an alarm just before sunrise, usually 5:30 or 6 a.m. depending on where you live and the time of year. Have everyone crawl out of bed and look toward the horizon. Then ooh and ahh at the flame-colored sun shooting into the sky.

WHAT YOU NEED

* DVDs or downloads that fit your theme

ONE HOUR OR MORE

BUILD-YOUR-OWN BARS

Girls gotta eat! Embrace fun with food by setting up bars for every meal. All you'll have to whip up are the basics—then put out some mini bowls of toppings and serving spoons, of course. Try these...

FRENCH TOAST BAR

YOGURT BAR

WHAT YOU NEED

* French toast
* Fresh berries
* Whipped cream
* Syrup
* Butter and jam
* Nutella

BREAKFAST

WHAT YOU NEED

* 2 to 4 different flavored yogurts
* Granola
* Fresh fruit
* Dried fruit
* Shaved coconut
* Chopped candy bars
* Chocolate chips
* Honey

SNACK

PASTA BAR

SODA FLOAT BAR

WHAT YOU NEED

DINNER

* 3 different types of cooked pasta
* Alfredo sauce
* Marinara sauce
* Pitted black olives
* Artichoke hearts
* Sundried tomatoes
* Mushrooms
* Peppers
* Onions
* Shredded or grated parmesan cheese

WHAT YOU NEED

DESSERT

* 2 to 4 different flavored ice creams
* 2 to 4 different flavored sodas
* 3 different flavored syrups
* Mini chocolate chips
* Maraschino cherries
* Whipped cream

THROW THE
BEST BASH

There's always a reason to celebrate—whether it's a birthday, a holiday or just an everyday! Playing hostess with the mostess just takes an ounce of organization, some proper planning and a festive attitude. Our gift to you? The party planning pointers ahead make it a piece of cake.

CHAPTER 6

CREATE A PHOTO BOOTH... OR A POP-UP VIDEO BOOTH

WHAT YOU NEED

* Plain white sheet
* Duct tape
* Painter's tape
* Box of props
  (try: colorful boas, zany hats, oversized glasses, lips on a stick)
* Mini chalkboards with chalk for guests to write messages
* Camera tripod
* Digital camera and remote shutter release

Mount the camera on the tripod and place it a few feet away from your sheeted wall. Frame the shot and angle the camera so no duct tape or outer wall space appears in the frame. You can ask a friend or a sibling to stand in front of your "booth" to help frame the shot.

Using painter's tape, make an X on the floor to mark the tripod's spot and the center and outer limits of where guests should stand for photos. Set up the remote shutter release and lay out your box of props and chalkboards before guests arrive.

Want to switch it up from standard pics? Have guests create a recorded message in your booth instead. Just switch the settings on your camera to video mode and let the creativity soar.

STYLE A 1-MINUTE CENTERPIECE

Make your tables the center of attention with this sweet eye candy. Fill empty vases with the candy of your choice, like conversation hearts or gumballs, and scatter the vases around the room. Want each table to be unique? Use jars of varying sizes and shapes to create different (but coordinating) confections.

WHAT YOU NEED

* Clear glass vases
* Colorful candy

BREAK THE ICE

Sometimes your guests won't know each other—and that can be part of the fun (hello, bestie matchmaking). Help everyone get comfy by starting friendly conversation as people stroll in.

TRY SOME OF THESE:

"So what did you do today?" It's the simplest of Qs but also the easiest to answer, since it doesn't require much thought.

"What does your name mean?" It summarizes the guest in a few words—and if they don't know the answer, ask them what they'd like their name to mean.

"If you could've invited a famous person as your party guest tonight, who would it be?" You'll get a quick glimpse at the guest's interests...and how creative he or she can be.

WHAT YOU NEED

* Willingness to speak up

DIY THE PERFECT PIÑATA

No party is ever complete without some swinging-for-surprises fun. Make your paste by combining a 50/50 mixture of water and glue in a bowl. Inflate your balloon, cut the newspaper into strips and start dipping and spreading. Begin with the body, covering most of the balloon but leaving a hole at the top, then branch out into whatever design you'd like. Let set. (Note: If you use a lot of layers, it can take overnight to dry, so give yourself plenty of time!) Pop the balloon with a pin, fill it up with candy and patch the hole. Dress it up with colorful tissue paper or paint, then hang it up and let the guests take a shot, er, swing.

WHAT YOU NEED

* Big balloon
* Pile of newspaper
* White glue
* Colored tissue paper or paint
* Candy variety pack
* Large bowl
* Fork to mix glue
* Safety pin

BUILD YOUR OWN

Sometimes the classics become even classier with a DIY touch.
Add your personal spin to these games.

TOTAL PLAYERS
2

TIC-TAC-WACKY

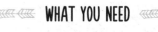

Make tic-tac-toe come to life. Clear out a space in the room and create a tic-tac-toe board using washi tape. You can make the board as big as you want, but make sure all nine boxes are wide enough to fit a plastic plate in each. Have each player pick a side. The guest who successfully lines up three of their colors in a straight or diagonal line first, wins.

WHAT YOU NEED

* Washi tape
* 5 red plastic plates
* 5 blue plastic plates

PARTY GAMES

PICK-ME-UP STICKS

TOTAL
PLAYERS

2+

WHAT YOU NEED

* 33 bamboo skewers
* 4 cans of spray paint (different colors)
* 1 can of black spray paint
* Newspaper

Seperate your skewers into 4 piles of 8 skewers, then lay them flat on newspaper in an area where you can use spray paint. Paint each group a different color, then lay out one lone skewer and paint it black. Let them all dry completely.

During the party, drop the bunch of sticks on a flat surface (try a tabletop or a clear spot on the carpet). Assign a point system for each color. For example, purple sticks are 2 points, red sticks are 4, green sticks are 6 and yellow sticks are 8.

Each player must use her fingers or the black stick to pull, push or roll away a single stick from the pile without disturbing (read: moving) any other stick. When she successfully steals one from the pile, she keeps it and continues removing sticks until she causes a secondary stick to move. Once all of the sticks have been picked up, each player adds up her score and the person with the most points wins.

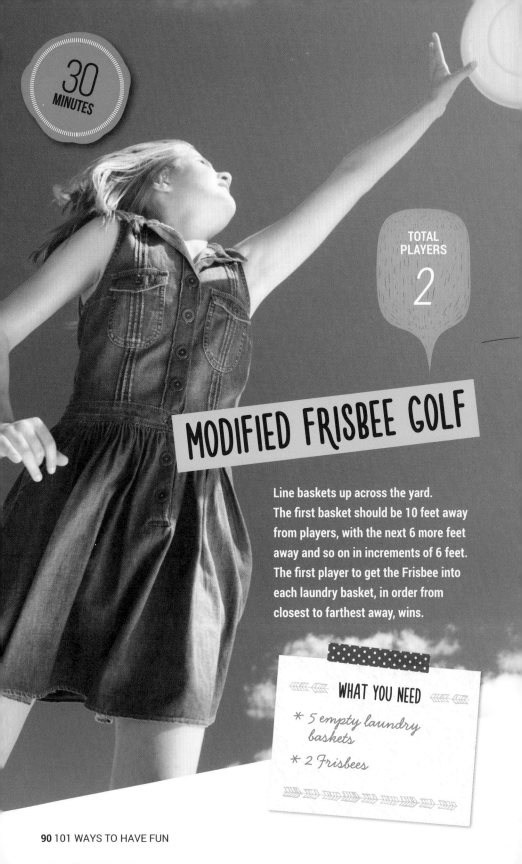

30 MINUTES

TOTAL PLAYERS
2

MODIFIED FRISBEE GOLF

Line baskets up across the yard. The first basket should be 10 feet away from players, with the next 6 more feet away and so on in increments of 6 feet. The first player to get the Frisbee into each laundry basket, in order from closest to farthest away, wins.

WHAT YOU NEED

* 5 empty laundry baskets
* 2 Frisbees

HOST YOUR OWN CUPCAKE WARS

WHAT YOU NEED

* Baked vanilla, chocolate and strawberry cupcakes (a dozen of each)
* Variety of flavored icings
* Variety of flavored puddings for cupcake fillings
* Assortment of hard toppings like sprinkles, nuts, chocolate chips
* Three surprise ingredients (like gummy worms, bacon, or sea salt)
* Paper and pens
* Utensils like spoons and butter knives

Give those TV chefs a run for their bakeries by testing all willing party guests. Have players break into teams of three or four. Pick a theme, like under the sea or outer space, and tell players they must make a delicious creation to reflect the theme.

Then reveal your three surprise ingredients and say they must use at least two in their creation. Let teams know they will be judged on three categories: taste, creativity and presentation.

Allow teams to brainstorm their designs with a pen and paper for 7 minutes before starting the clock. Teams can grab five baked cupcakes (they'll need to make three decorated cupcakes for the judges to taste, but can also have two extras for backup), and all of the toppings, fillings and utensils needed to make their treat.

When time's up (say, 20 to 25 minutes) teams must have their three decorated cupcakes placed on individual plates and ready to present.

Have your judges score each cupcake on taste, creativity and presentation, tally up the points and crown the cupcake queens.

THROW A MYSTERY BASH

Dress it

Tape cutout footprints on the floor from the front door leading into the dining room. As each guest comes in, give them a bag filled with a small plastic magnifying glass, pad of paper, pen and handmade detective badge.

Serve it

Dole out chocolate-frosted cupcakes with a big question mark piped on top, frosted donuts with a stick at each bottom to look like magnifying glasses and "mystery" purple punch (equal parts grape juice and ginger ale).

Do it

Play "Gotcha!" Divide your friends into two groups—burglars and guests—by having everyone select a piece of paper from a hat that also names a specific object you placed in the room (like a watch or a nail polish). As your party plays out, the burglars must sneakily steal their assigned item. Once all treasures have turned up missing, each guest must use their detective skills to guess which thief palmed their prize.

HOST A PINK PARTY

Dress it

Have guests come dressed in head-to-toe pink. Decorate the snack table with palette-appropriate gummies and flowers.

Serve it

Indulge in rosy-colored fizzy sips (mix 2/3 pink lemonade and 1/3 seltzer) and pink-frosted strawberry cupcakes.

Do it

Set up a pink mani/pedi station and rock out to a pink-themed playlist, then watch the always classic flick *Pretty in Pink*.

FUN WAYS TO
MAKE $ FAST

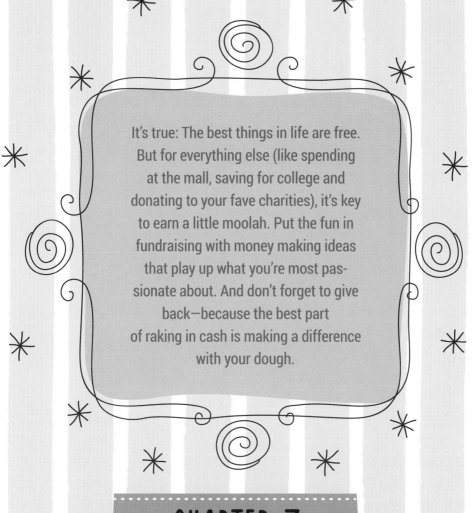

It's true: The best things in life are free. But for everything else (like spending at the mall, saving for college and donating to your fave charities), it's key to earn a little moolah. Put the fun in fundraising with money making ideas that play up what you're most passionate about. And don't forget to give back—because the best part of raking in cash is making a difference with your dough.

CHAPTER 7

POP QUIZ:
WHAT'S YOUR WORK STYLE?

Social vs. Independent
A. I get in my own zone and love to work solo

B. I'm most creative when collaborating with my crew

Sprint vs. Marathon
A. I like bouncing around and working in bursts

B. I buckle down and knock my work out at once

Make It vs. Do It
A. I love design, DIY, crafting and cooking

B. I'm organized, ambitious and professional

Expert vs. Teacher
A. I always get compliments on things I make

B. I'm a pro at teaching things to my friends

MOSTLY A's
You might be great at making something and selling it to others. Check out pages 98 and 107 for inspiration.

MOSTLY B's
You'd be good at selling a service to people. Get started with ideas mentioned on pages 99 and 101.

FILL A BAD HABIT BANK

You swore you'd never bite your nails again. But then, well... you know. Make a list of bad mannerisms (like cracking your knuckles or procrastinating on school projects), then keep one copy in your bag and give one to a trusted friend who promises to call you out if she sees you pulling a no-no.

For every instance you perform a bad habit, charge yourself a penny for the first time that day, followed by a nickel the second time and so on in increments of five cents.

When you eventually kick your habits to the curb (congrats!), make up new "taxes" for yourself—like forgetting to make your bed or saying something negative.

WHAT YOU NEED

* Piggy bank or empty vase
* Coins

CRAFT GREETING CARDS

30 MINUTES

PER BUNDLE

$9

WHAT YOU NEED

* Solid-colored stationery in bulk
* Matching envelopes in bulk
* Ink pads, stencils, glitter, stickers, colored pencils
* Cute ribbon from your family's closet

Have an artsy side? Make others smile (while you make money!) and design your own greeting cards. Fold paper in half and decorate front with your supplies. You can opt for seasonal selections like Christmas or birthdays. Create funny covers with words inside to match, or keep it timeless with beautiful cover designs and a blank message inside.

Tie ribbon around bundles of 10 to 15 card and envelope sets, then sell them to friends and fam. Let the word-of-mouth recommendations begin!

START A DOG WALKING BIZ

There are plenty of lonely pooches whose owners have to work crazy long hours. Knock on your neighbors' doors and offer to give those four-legged friends a special stroll every afternoon.

Walk the dogs right when you get home from school Monday through Friday (set an alarm on your phone so you remember). Be sure you have all special instructions and emergency contact info on hand for each dog. Pack plenty of treats (for when the pups are sweet) and baggies (to, ahem, clean up as you go).

Have more than one dog client? Don't walk too many at the same time or risk being walked by them. Pair up dogs that you know will get along, and break your strolls into a few shifts.

PER DOG PER WEEK

$10-$15

WHAT YOU NEED

* Pups from your neighborhood
* House keys
* Selection of leashes
* Doggie treats
* Pet waste bags

TALK TECH

O K, you iPhone/MacBook/Facebook/
Twitter pro. You're practically wired
to navigate anything with an On
button or WiFi connection, so use
those smartie skills to your advantage.

An elderly neighbor just got his first
smartphone or laptop? Offer to show him the
ropes. Swing by local businesses (like your
fave fro-yo spot) and ask if you can be their
social media manager, or offer your services
to a nonprofit for free.

Print flyers describing the tech-related
services you offer, and don't forget to include
any accolades (like your impressive number
of Twitter followers or that special computer
class you aced in school). Also add your
phone number and custom business email
address (make sure your parents can monitor
it) so interested clients can get in touch
about rates and dates. Drop off your flyers at
every house in your neighborhood and pass
one out to every manager at stores. Finally,
ask friends and fam to spread the word.

*$10 PER HOUR FOR TRAINING,
$15 PER HOUR FOR SOCIAL
MEDIA MANAGEMENT*

$10-$15

WHAT YOU NEED

* *Your digital savviness*

BECOME A TEACHER

PER HOUR-LONG SESSION (DEPENDING ON THE SKILL)

$15

So you know how to do a kickin' backflip or have perfected the sweet sound of a cello? Use your skills to school others on the talent they've been itching to learn.

Post your services in the church bulletin or have your parents consult their social and professional circles for leads. Just be sure you agree upfront on who's responsible for toting equipment and where the lessons will take place.

As a trial run, offer a 30-minute sample session for a fraction of the cost. This way both you and the client will see if it's a good match before moving forward with weekly lessons.

WHAT YOU NEED

* A hobby you're skilled in
* Any required equipment

HAVE A YARD SALE

It's time to make cash off of that trash (well, gently used things you no longer love). Get your folks in on the plan and ask if you can sell random stuff your family could stand to part with (check the garage and attic!).

Organize everything by categories: clothes, books, knickknacks, furniture and so on. Using your cardboard and markers, make signs announcing the sale (include your address, the date and the time) and tape them on street poles around the neighborhood.

On the day of the sale, get up early and start laying things out on your table. Use your fence or a coatrack to display clothes and accessories. Ask your parents to do a final sweep to make sure nothing was accidentally put out. Then take your painter's tape and marker and start placing a price tag on every item.

During the sale, be sure to wear an outfit with good pockets or sport a cross-body bag so you have money on hand to distribute change. Some people might "haggle" you, meaning they'll try talking you down from your marked price. If that's the case, just remember to be flexible and remain friendly—especially considering it's stuff you don't want anyway.

When the sale is over, pack up and ask Mom or Dad to help you take any leftover items to a charity. No matter how much money you make, you'll feel great knowing the house is now an uncluttered, happy place.

WHAT YOU NEED

* Everything in your closet you haven't worn in over two years
* Knickknacks, stuffed animals, toys with no sentimental value
* Stuff your parents don't need anymore
* Blue painter's tape
* Table and chairs
* Cardboard, masking tape and markers

YARD SALE

PRICE VARIES IF THE PIECE IS STURDY AND MADE OF REAL WOOD

$.25-$5
FOR CLOTHING

$1 - $3
FOR BOOKS, DVDS, TOYS AND GAMES

$15-$35
FOR FURNITURE

$1 - $4
FOR KITCHEN STUFF

ONE HOUR OR MORE

SET UP A STAND

The likelihood of competing with other lemonade stands might be high—especially in the summertime. Give new flair to the same ol', same ol' by picking a different theme. Set up shop with your table and chairs right in front of your house (this way you can quickly replenish essentials if needed). Don't live in a high-traffic area? Ask to use a friend's more desirable location and split the profit.

Make bright and bold signs to promote the details of your specialized stand. Don't be afraid to use social media—or ask pals to post about it—to spread the word, too. Try these themes...

WHAT YOU NEED

* Table and chairs
* Colorful poster board and markers
* Tape
* Shoebox with enough change to break bills
* Additional required material based on theme

SPRITZER STAND

WHAT YOU NEED

- Pitcher of fresh-squeezed lemonade
- Seltzer
- Wooden spoon
- Plastic cups
- Cooler filled with sealable bags of ice and cold freezer packs

PER CUP

$1

We heart this fizzier version to the sweet classic—and know your customers will, too. Keep bottles of seltzer and ice in your cooler. When someone drops by, fill half the cup with lemonade and half with seltzer. Stir, drop in a few cubes and serve. Yum!

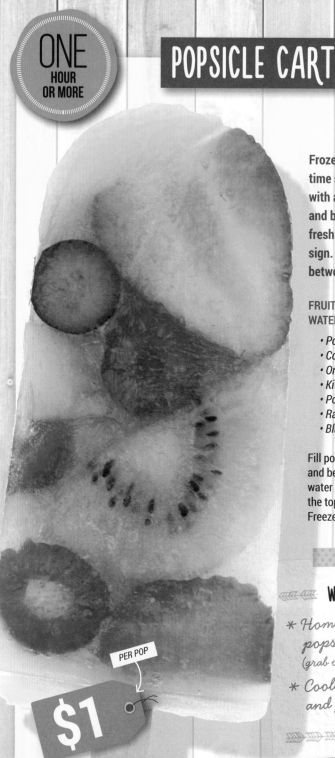

POPSICLE CART

Frozen treats are a summer-time smash. Fill your cooler with a batch of pretty pops and be sure to include your fresh flavors on a standout sign. Freeze any leftovers between selling sessions!

FRUITY COCONUT WATER POPSICLE

- *Popsicle molds*
- *Coconut water*
- *Orange slices*
- *Kiwi slices*
- *Pomegranate seeds*
- *Raspberries*
- *Blueberries*

Fill popsicle molds with fruit and berries. Pour in coconut water (leaving some space at the top). Pop in a wooden stick. Freeze at least 2 hours.

WHAT YOU NEED

* *Homemade fruity popsicles* (grab our recipe above)
* *Cooler filled with ice and freezer packs*

PER POP

$1

SEASONAL SWEETS BOOTH

Create a mini menu of 2-3 seasonal or holiday treats to sell. Keep the snacks simple and the themes creative. While everyone might love a pie at Thanksgiving, those can be complicated to make. Instead, opt for pumpkin breads or cookies, which are super easy to bake up...but lots of people don't have time to make them, and that's where you come in!

PER 3 COOKIES

$2

When Christmas rolls around? Whip up your best sugar cookies or a favorite family treat. If it's not too cold, get bundled up and lure them with hot cocoa. If the temps are too arctic, opt for the door-to-door option, making sure to only knock where you know the neighbors. Don't forget sprinkles!

WHAT YOU NEED

* Homemade desserts
* Napkins, baggies or plastic wrap

RAKE IN THE BUCKS

Want to get paid for working out? Welcome to the world of yard work, a dirty job (literally!) that'll earn you fresh air, exercise and, yep, money. Hit your neighborhood and offer to rake up leaves in the fall or weed gardens in the spring.

Just remember, outdoor work can be tough—so wear plenty of sunscreen, stay hydrated and bring some extra snacks. One more thing to pack? Headphones and an awesome playlist!

WHAT YOU NEED

* Rake
* Plastic trash bags
* Gardening gloves

$10-$15
PER HOUR

SN-APP IT UP

It's fun to see your savings soar! Managing your money and setting goals for big gifts can be a blast when it comes in cute app form. Try these faves!

2K Money (iOS)

This app's wishlist feature reminds you that you've got your eye on—and how saving your pennies along the way can add up to something awesome.

bankaroo (iOS and Android)

Made by a kid for kids, this app helps track your birthday money, chore cash and allowance all separately...so you know exactly where it all went.

A+Allowance (iOS)

Set up this simple chore chart to know what you're working for, then sort it with the 10/10/10/70 system—10% giving, 10% investing, 10% saving and 70% fun.

Toshl Finance (iOS and Android)

Plan ahead by tracking future expenses compared to this month's moola, and let informative graphs paint you the bigger bucks picture.

GET ACTIVE

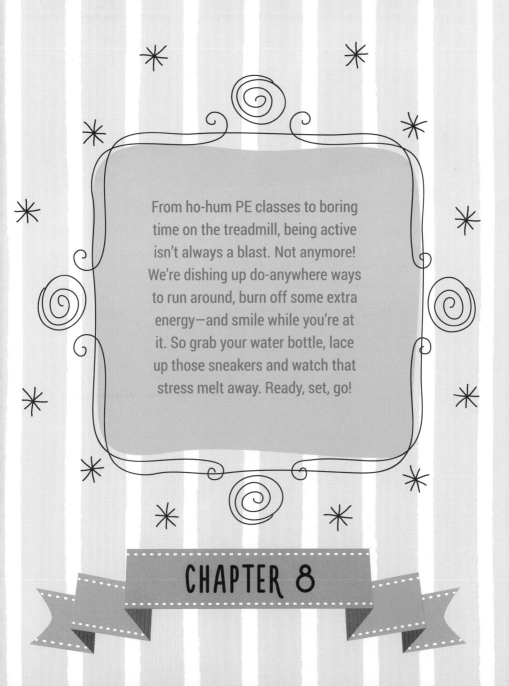

From ho-hum PE classes to boring time on the treadmill, being active isn't always a blast. Not anymore! We're dishing up do-anywhere ways to run around, burn off some extra energy—and smile while you're at it. So grab your water bottle, lace up those sneakers and watch that stress melt away. Ready, set, go!

CHAPTER 8

HOST A DIY DANCE MARATHON
(SORT OF!)

Get goofy one Saturday afternoon by setting your phone alarm for every hour of the day. When the buzzer chimes? Shake it off! Boogie down like no one is watching (hint: playing a song off YouTube can help you find the beat). Dancing is a proven mood booster, and those good vibes will last long after your last move of the day.

WHAT YOU NEED

* A phone or watch with an alarm
* Music

HOP YOUR WAY TO HEALTHY

Jumping rope is secretly super healthy—it's amazing for your heart and works your entire body. But you don't have to be a Double Dutch pro to bounce your way to those benefits. Head to the garage and find your old rope, then do a little warm-up (like hopping in place or skipping around your backyard). Finally, grab onto those handles and give it all you've got...for about 5 to 8 minutes. Skipping rope is hard, though, so don't feel like you have to hop to it for an hour.

WHAT YOU NEED

* Workout clothes
* Sneakers
* Jump rope

JOG A FUNSY 5K

Using an app like Google Maps or MapMyRun, figure out a 5K route for your just-you "race," then lace up your sneakers and hit the road. It's as simple as going slowly, taking deep breaths and walking when necessary. (Hey, a combo of running and walking is totally cool in this case...there's no real timer. No sense in pushing it.) Need a little extra motivation? Dedicate your route to a cause...and promise yourself if you complete the course, you'll donate the next $10 you earn to a favorite charity. Give yourself a big high five at the finish, and don't forget to drink plenty of water. You'll likely be tired—but it'll be worth it.

WHAT YOU NEED

* Exercise clothes
* Sneakers
* Water
* Access to a 3-mile loop
  (like a track or a safe stretch
  of road that has a sidewalk)

FLIP YOUR WORLD

There's something pretty awesome about being head over heels...and it can be good for your body, too. Amazingly, you don't have to ride on a loop-de-loop rollercoaster or sign up for gymnastics lessons to get that same rush.

Doing bridges—those rainbow-shaped bendy tricks—can be a great way to stretch your whole body and give your brain perspective. If you haven't mastered the big one (like in the pic), try out a Pilates baby bridge...

1. Lie back with your knees bent, your feet flat and arms by your sides. Raise your hips off the mat, keeping your core tight.

2. Inhale as you straighten and lift your right leg, making sure not to let your hip drop.

3. Slowly exhale and extend your leg up toward the ceiling, keeping your hips level and your core tight.

4. Return your leg to the starting position and switch to your left leg. Repeat five times on each leg.

WHAT YOU NEED

* Comfy clothes
* A clear space on carpet (or a yoga mat)
* Bare feet

GO WITH

Whether you need to wake up in the a.m. or just zap the blahs whenever, an invigorating yoga flow can get the blood moving (while still calming your mind). Tara Stiles, yoga instructor and owner of Strala Yoga, shows how to do these poses. Repeat on both sides a few times every week (staying in each pose for 3 to 5 breaths) to feel less stressed.

1. STANDING FORWARD BEND Inhale and lift your arms up over your head. Exhale and fold forward. Interlace your fingers behind your back, straighten your arms and relax your shoulders.

2. PLANK Get into push-up position. Use your ab and glute muscles to stay straight, and don't let your belly dip.

3. UP DOG Start in a plank. Uncurl your toes (you'll support yourself on the tops of your feet), lower your rear end down and let your back arch. Relax your shoulders and lift your chest up.

4. DOWN DOG Place your hands and feet on the ground. Lift your hips up so your body makes an inverted "V" shape.

5. DOWN DOG SPLIT WITH OPEN HIPS From down dog, inhale and lift your right leg behind you. Open your hips and shoulders to face the right and bend your knee behind you to open the hips even more.

THE FLOW

6. DOWN DOG SPLIT WITH SQUARE HIPS Keep the right leg lifted high and square off your hips, so the toes point down toward the ground.

7. KNEE TO FOREHEAD From the down dog split, lift your right knee and try to touch it to your forehead.

8. LOW LUNGE Place your right foot between your hands for a lunge.

9. WARRIOR III From the low lunge, shift your weight onto your right leg and stand up. Extend your left leg behind you. If you feel stable, reach your arms out in front of you. Wobbly? Keep your fingers on the floor.

10. TREE
While standing on your right leg, grab your left ankle and press it into your upper thigh. Reach your arms over your head or keep your hands clasped in front of your heart. Repeat the routine on the other side.

WHAT YOU NEED

* Comfy clothes or PJs
* A clear space that's about 5 feet long
* A sense of calm

ONE
HOUR
OR MORE

WHAT YOU NEED

* An activity you love
* Exercise clothes
* A journal (optional)

FEEL BEA-YOU-TI-FUL

We've been lucky enough to talk to tons of athletes who are at the top of their game. And guess what? It's not the medals and titles that make them feel like all-stars. So many pros have said that staying active helps them with their body confidence...and helps them feel gorgeous inside and out.

Alex Morgan, former U.S. Olympic soccer player, confessed that she struggled with body image until she started playing sports. "I had to find something that gave me confidence and helped me feel beautiful," she says. "You feel so much better about yourself when you're doing something you love."

So what's a normal girl to do? Simply carve out 30 minutes a day to dedicate to your mind, body and spirit. Start with an activity you love, like archery, basketball, biking, climbing, dancing, field hockey, gymnastics, hiking, running, pilates, paddleboarding, soccer, spinning, swimming, walking, yoga or zumba. (Whew. Or whatever you want to add to this list!) Sure, it's hard to play a full-on team sport solo, but you can always work on your skills or do the same warmup your coach has you perform in practice. Don't have a special thing you love quite yet? Work your way down the list above or check out a class at the local Y.

We're not saying you have to run 10 miles every morning, but getting yourself out for a solid 30 minutes a day is key to a beautiful mind-set. "The easiest way to love your body is to live as healthily as possible," says Olympic gold metal gymnast Gabby Douglas.

To track how you feel post-sweat, it can be helpful to keep a "healthy mind, healthy body" journal. Write down what you did for exercise and what's going on in your head after exercising. And then on days when you want to skip, flip back to your pages and remember why you started moving in the first place.

GET CRAFTY

Spending a crafternoon with your BFFs
is the best—everyone can chill out with
lemonade and create the prettiest DIYs.
The how-tos ahead are perfect for those
Insta-worthy bonding moments...
but they're also just as fun to whip up
when you have a free night and want
to relax. Best yet? They're easy enough
for darlings new to DIY, but stylish
enough for pro craftinistas.

CHAPTER 9

GIRLY VOTIVES

WHAT YOU NEED

* 3 small glass votive candle holders

* 3 small votive candles

* Washi tape in a variety of 3-4 colors (find it at a craft store)

* Scissors

1. Measure a piece of tape to fit around the circumference of the glass votive.

2. Trim tape where ends meet and affix to glass, making sure to keep the tape line straight.

3. Repeat with another pattern/color of Washi tape 2 to 3 times, so you have multiple rows of tape.

4. Insert a candle and get glowing! Remember to be careful if you're using matches. (Not allowed to have candles in your room? Pick up no-flame, battery-operated candle-shaped cuties at the craft store.)

CONFETTI CARDS

1. Use the hole punch to cut out lots of small circles from the gold vinyl paper.

2. Peel the backing off your vinyl dots and affix to the front of the card.

3. Space them out evenly or randomly, spell out your friend's name or make a pretty design—it's up to you.

WHAT YOU NEED

* Folded, plain card-stock and matching envelopes

* Hole punch

* Gold vinyl paper (find on amazon.com)

30 MINUTES

MERCI BEAUCOUP PULLOVER

1. Set your iron to a dry-heat setting. Lay the sweatshirt on the ironing board, and lay out the letters on the front where you want them.

2. Remove paper backing if there is any and affix letters to the shirt. Place the dish towel over letters and press iron down for 15 seconds.

3. Turn shirt inside out and press iron down on reverse side of letters for 25 seconds.

4. Repeat steps 2 and 3 as needed until letters are set in place.

WHAT YOU NEED

* Sweatshirt
* Iron-on letters
* Iron and ironing board
* Clean dish towel

MINI METALLIC PAINT CHIP PRETTIES

1. Using an upside-down water glass, trace a circle onto a piece of lightweight cardboard. Cut out cardboard circle so you're left with a square of cardboard with a negative circle in the center. Use this as your stencil.

2. Trace the circle stencil onto the reverse side of each paint chip. Cut out the circle carefully using scissors.

3. Punch a hole in each circle about ¼-inch from the edge.

4. Thread a paint chip onto the cord and knot around the hole to lock in place. Repeat. Chips should be 6 inches apart.

WHAT YOU NEED

* 3 yards metallic cord

* 20 metallic paint chips
  (try the Martha Stewart Living collection from Home Depot)

* 2 ½-inch circle stencil
  (make one with the bottom of a glass and cardstock)

* Pen

* Scissors

* Hole punch

PAINT A SUNSET

1. About 20 minutes before sunset (check online for the exact time in your area), set up your "workshop" facing west.

2. Look around carefully to get a sense of the surroundings. What's the landscape like?

3. Lightly sketch what you see. Later, you'll paint over this initial drawing.

4. Begin to paint the landscape. Aim to catch the colors at their best, which will be a little later in the sun-setting process.

5. Keep adding color until you've painted a scene that inspires you. Remember: Some artists work in a more realistic fashion and others keep it abstract —it's fun to play with both.

WHAT YOU NEED

* Paints, either water-colors or acrylics
* Paintbrushes
* Pencils
* Glass of water
* Paper towels
* Thick paper or a canvas (you can buy either at a craft store)

CREATE A GALLERY WALL

1. First, ask your parents for permission to hang pictures on your wall. It'll create some banging and leave small holes in the wall. If they say no, proceed by taping unframed pics in the same gallery-style fashion.

2. Lay out the pictures on your floor and arrange them in a way that you love. To create a real gallery-wall feel, the pictures should be clustered kind of close together, but not necessarily in straight lines.

3. Start by hanging or taping up the center picture, and work your way out.

4. Stand back and admire your work!

WHAT YOU NEED

* Pictures
* Frames
* Washi tape or a hammer and nails

**CRAFT, FASHION AND
BEAUTY PHOTOGRAPHY:**

SEAN SCHEIDT
52-53, 55

**THE BEAUTY
DEPARTMENT**
54

BRION MCCARTHY
61-62, 65 122-125